Up the Learning Tree

by *Marcia Vaughan*

illustrated by

Derek Blanks

Lee & Low Books Inc.
New York

LEE & LOW BOOKS Inc., 95 Madison Avenue, New York, NY 10016
leeandlow.com

Sources for Quotations:
Cornelius, Janet Duitsman. *When I Can Read My Title Clear: Literacy, Slavery, and
    Religion in the Antebellum South.* Columbia, SC: University of South Carolina Press, 1991.
Hurmence, Belinda, ed. *Before Freedom, When I Just Can Remember: Twenty-seven Oral
    Histories of Former South Carolina Slaves.* Winston-Salem, NC: John F. Blair, 1989.

Manufactured in China

Book design by Christy Hale
Book production by The Kids at Our House

The text is set in Bell
The illustrations are rendered in oil paint

10 9 8 7 6 5 4 3
First Edition

Library of Congress Cataloging-in-Publication Data
Vaughan, Marcia K.
Up the learning tree / by Marcia Vaughan ; illustrated by Derek Blanks.— 1st ed.
    p. cm.
Summary: A young slave boy risks his life to learn how to read, and with the
unsuspecting help of a teacher from the North, begins to realize his dream.
ISBN 1-58430-049-3
[1. Reading—Fiction. 2. Learning—Fiction. 3. Slavery—Fiction. 4. African Americans—
Fiction. 5. Teachers—Fiction.] I. Blanks, Derek, ill. II. Title.
PZ7.V452 Up 2003
[E]—dc21   2002030166

*W*ith love and appreciation for
Renae Taylor, Jan Smith, Carolyn Buehl, Jon Torgerson,
Nancy Alley, Bonnie Campbell-Hill, and Lisa Blau,
extraordinary teachers who touch the hearts of their students
and inspire a life-long love of learning—M.V.

*F*or my beautiful wife and loving family.
Thanks for your love and support throughout this project—D.B.

My name's Henry Bell. Never been to school
myself. Book learning's not allowed for slaves.
Master Grismore says he'll take an ax to the finger
of any slave who touches a book.

I'm too busy working in the yard and helping
in the fields to give learning much thought till the
morning Mistress calls me to the big house.

"Henry," Mistress says to me, "Little Master Simon will be going to school at the schoolhouse down the road. I want you to walk him to and from school every day and take him his lunch. You think you're smart enough to do that?"

"Yes, ma'am," I answer, my face not showing how her words sting. Mama says Master and Mistress think we are dull-minded, but I know different. Before Pap got sold away, he told me book learning would help us escape slavery. That's why white folks don't allow slaves to learn to read.

There must be something powerful in books, and I want to know what it is.

After walking Simon to school the next day, I carry wood to the kitchen for the big house and pull weeds along the fence. I work fast and get back to the schoolhouse early. I scoot up the sycamore tree just as the door opens and the teacher leads the children outside to sit in the shade. She talks different, not like folks round here. Children call her Miss Hattie.

Miss Hattie carries a book. My heart pounds as she opens it up. Never heard anybody read a book before. I hold my breath as her eyes glide across the page. Like magic, a story about things called dragons and castles comes pouring out of her mouth. In my life I never heard anything like that!

Right then I get it in my heart to learn to read, and I get it in my head ain't nothing going to stop me.

I do my work lickety-split every day after that, then race to the sycamore tree. Peeking between the leaves, I see Miss Hattie. She talks loud and clear as the morning bell.

"This letter is *A*," she says, making a pointed shape on a board.

"*A*," the children say.

"*A*," says me, soft and low.

"Now, write the letter *A* on your slate," Miss Hattie says.

Don't have no slate, so I carve that letter into the soft bark of the tree. Closing my eyes, I run my finger up, down, and across that *A* till I can see it in my head.

Glory be, I got a letter of my very own!

Every day I watch Miss Hattie. Soon I know five letters. Then one day she shows the children how to string those letters together. All suddenlike, things begin working in my head. I know exactly what word those letters are going to make before Miss Hattie even says so!

I feel sparks dancing round inside me like a fire that's been fanned by the wind. I'm learning, just like those schoolchildren! One day sure I'll be able to read a book too.

Day after day I feel the power of learning come flying out of that schoolhouse and straight into my head. My mama would be so proud of me, but I can't tell her yet. Can't tell nobody. The thought of Master's ax reminds me to keep my learning secret.

Then cold old winter comes blowing in. No leaves on the sycamore tree to hide me now. I got to find some other way to learn.

Me and Master Simon get along fine. On the walk home I say, "What you learn today, Master Simon?"

Simon's busting his britches to tell me. "I learned to spell *big*," he boasts. *"B-I-G!"*

"Mercy me, you sure spell nice," I say. "Can you spell anything else?"

"I can spell *pig* and *dig*," Simon says. "I can write them too." Simon snatches up a stick and scratches the words in the road.

I lock them in my head. Next day I carve those words into the branches of the sycamore. Every day Simon teaches me something new. Before long my tree's got more words than a hoot owl has feathers.

Spring comes and with it the fever. Lots of folks sicken.
Some die. My friend Wilfred, who drives the buggy for
Mistress, falls bad sick. To keep Simon from catching the
fever, Mistress says he won't be going to school for a while.

My heart sinks like a rock tossed down the well. But then
Mistress says Simon will be doing his lessons at home. I'm
to carry them to and from school for the teacher to correct.

On my way, when I'm certain nobody can see me, I sneak
a peek at them lessons, grabbing every scrap of learning I can.

One day in the schoolhouse I see
a badly torn book in the trash. Miss
Hattie's busy checking Simon's work,
so fast as a fox I snatch up the book,
stuff it under my shirt, and hold it
tight to my chest. Hugging that book's
like hugging hope. I feel my heart
beating against it, and I know nothing
can stop me from learning now.

Suddenly a shadow falls at my feet.

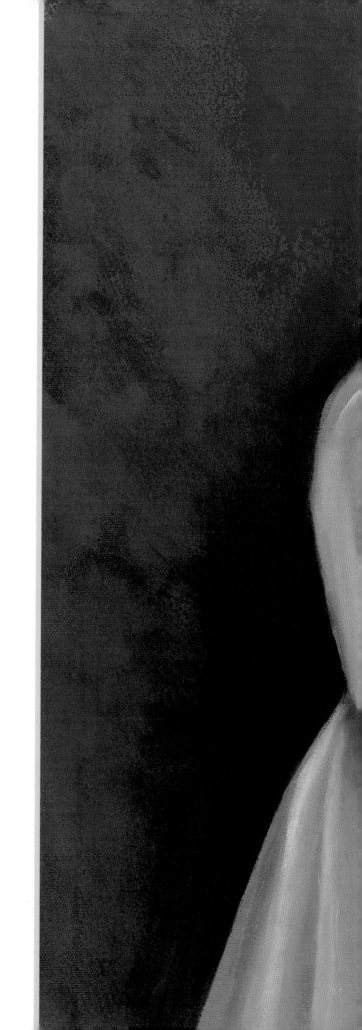

"What's your name?" Miss Hattie asks.

"Henry Bell, ma'am," I mumble.

"Henry, what are you aiming to do with that book you've got hidden under your shirt?"

I take a deep breath. "I was going to learn to read it, ma'am."

"You know Master Grismore does not allow his slaves to be educated," she says. "You could be severely punished."

"But I got to learn to read, 'cause if I do then maybe one day I can get myself free." The words come pouring out of my mouth before I can stop them.

Miss Hattie looks at me long and hard. "Henry," she says. "I don't believe in slavery or in keeping people ignorant. If you're willing to take such a big risk, then I am too. You keep that book. Just be careful. I like my job, and I don't want to lose it."

"Yes, Miss Hattie," I say. "I like my fingers and don't want to lose them neither." Then I hurry toward the door.

"Henry," she calls after me. "If Simon has any questions about his schoolwork, you be sure and tell me."

I smile 'cause I'm thinking when she says Simon, she means me!

Every afternoon after that if no one's around, Miss Hattie helps me with my learning. Some days we work on words and letters. Other days she teaches me numbers, and before long I can do sums.

"Henry, there's something special I'd like you to see," Miss Hattie tells me one day. She unrolls a large piece of paper covered with strange shapes.

"This is a map of the world. You live here in America. Across this big ocean is Africa, where your ancestors lived in freedom before they were taken as slaves."

Never knew the world was so big, but I'd heard Mama and Pap talk about Africa. I look at that map for a long time, etching the picture of Africa into my memory.

Suddenly I get an idea.

"Miss Hattie," I say. "There's something special I'd like you to see too. Can you climb a tree?"

Miss Hattie nods yes, so I help her up through the branches of the sycamore tree. Her eyes grow big as she runs her fingers over my words.

"Henry, this is remarkable," Miss Hattie says. "This tree is like a giant book you've written all by yourself. In all my years of teaching, I've never had a student as determined to learn as you."

Next day is Friday. After the children have gone, I go into the schoolhouse with Simon's lessons.

"I have something for you, Henry," Miss Hattie says. Opening a drawer, she takes out a brand spankin' new book and puts it in my hands.

"It's about Africa," she says.

My heart leaps like a wild horse. A new book of my very own!

The door squeaks. We both jump.

One of the schoolgirls stands in the doorway. "What's that slave boy doing in here?" she says, scowling.

"He's taking lessons to Simon Grismore," Miss Hattie says. "Why are you here, Ginny?"

"I forgot my speller. I come to fetch it," the girl answers.

"That's fine," says Miss Hattie. "You get your book and hurry on home before your mother frets."

"Yes, ma'am," the girl answers, a suspicious look flashing across her face.

After she leaves Miss Hattie walks me to the door. "Henry, you remember now, be careful."

Come Monday afternoon I'm sitting on a limb of the sycamore, turning the pages of my new book. Suddenly I hear riders coming like thunder up the road. Three men stop at the schoolhouse. My heart turns cold. Tall man's got an ax tied to his saddle.

Miss Hattie comes to the door. Tall man's only half off his horse when he starts shouting, "You no-account troublemaker! My girl says you been teaching a slave."

Miss Hattie throws back her shoulders. "I have indeed," she says.

Tall man storms right up to her. "What's his name?" he snaps, pulling back his fist.

Miss Hattie looks him straight in the eye. "He's from the Grismore plantation," she says. "His name is . . . Wilfred."

I can't believe my ears. Fever took Wilfred last Saturday.

Tall man knows this too. "We'll be back tomorrow," he threatens. "You better be gone. No telling what might happen if you're not." Then those men ride off fast as they came.

I wait a long time before I climb down the sycamore and slip into the schoolhouse. Miss Hattie's taking things out of her desk.

"You got to go?" I ask even though I already know the answer.

"Yes, Henry, I do."

"Why'd you teach me, Miss Hattie?" I ask. "Why'd you teach a slave like me?"

"Henry, you know I believe everyone has a right to learn. Your body may be bound by slavery, but your mind is free. Someday I hope you'll be free to learn whatever your heart desires."

Down deep I am hoping the very same thing.

"I'm going to keep on learning, Miss Hattie," I say. "I can do it. I know I can."

She nods her head. "I believe you, Henry. Yes, I do."

I know I'll never see Miss Hattie again. Then all suddenlike I get an idea. I scramble up the sycamore and break off a branch with my writing on it.

"This is for you, Miss Hattie," I say, holding out the branch. "So's you won't forget me."

She runs her fingers over the letters, then hugs me tight. "Henry, as long as I live, I will never forget you."

And I keep my word to
Miss Hattie. I keep learning
every chance I get.
My name's Henry Bell. I got it in my
heart to learn, and I got it in my head ain't
nothing going to stop me.

DURING THE DAYS OF SLAVERY in the United States (1619–1865), enslaved people were considered property. They had no rights and were forced to work and obey the rules set by their owners. Many owners kept their slaves ignorant and illiterate because they feared literate slaves would write their own passes to leave the plantation and escape to freedom in the North.

The idea for *Up the Learning Tree* came to me while I was reading the oral histories of former slaves. Even though enslaved people who were found with reading or writing materials were severely punished, the desire to learn was strong. Those caught with books, newspapers, or items for writing might be sold off, whipped, or have one or more fingers cut off. Still, learning to read and write was of great importance to those who were enslaved, and they often devised clever ways to go about learning so their owners would not know.

> *"I was small in slavery time, and played with the white chaps. Once [Marster] saw me and some other chaps, white chaps, under a tree playing with letter blocks. They had the ABCs on them. Marster got awful mad and got off his horse and whipped me good."*
> —MILTON MARSHALL
> from *Before Freedom, When I Just Can Remember*

> *"De say we git smarter den dey was if we learn anything, but we slips around and gits hold of dat Webster's old blue back speller and we hides it til way in de night and den we ights a little pine torch and studies dat spellin' book. We learn it too."*
> —JENNY PROCTOR
> from *When I Can Read My Title Clear*

Being educated helped enslaved people in their quest for self-worth and dignity, while the ability to learn about the outside world helped them in their quest for freedom. In *Up the Learning Tree* I wanted to bring this passion for learning to life through the experiences of a young boy who triumphs over serious dangers and obstacles and learns to read and write.

> *"Once you learn to read you will be forever free."*
> —FREDERICK DOUGLASS